MANY MUSINGS

of a

MEANDERING MIND

A collection of Flash Fiction and Poems

By

Egon S Frank

Other publications by Egon S Frank:

A Handful of Egon: Cookbook 1 –

A Collection of Sips, Noshes & Musings

Another Handful of Egon: Cookbook 2 – More Noshes

Danube River Cruise

egon.frank@gmail.com.

Foreword

For many years, I've been a scribbler, which started, more or less, when I was about 16 years old. While still in high school, I penned my first fictional story, which was published in our school newspaper. It was a hit, and I was hooked on writing. That story is now called "The Unexpected," followed by "The Job."

Much of what I have penned over the years has been based, but not always, on events that have affected me personally in one way or another, which I then converted into narratives. Some stories originated as the result of some new articles. Others are pure fiction.

And while I have written many reports and proposals in the past for work and some stories for self-entertainment, I was suddenly informed that a number of my scribbles, including first-person narratives, were NOT short stories but were labeled as flash fiction.

This was news to me. I always used to categorize my writings as a short story, an essay, or a rant. Apparently, a demarcation was established by those in power, starting with Grimm's' Fairytales and Aesop's Fables, as follows:

Microfiction	100 – 500 words
Sudden Fiction	750 words
Flash Fiction	up to 1,500 words

Meanwhile, I simply continue to hum along, leaving some scratches on some vellum – well, on my computer - to express a thought or two or to tell a story in either prose or a narrative. This section contains a number of my flash fiction efforts, most of which fall into one of the forgoing categories.

I dedicate this effort to my dear wife, Pamela, for her perseverance and for putting up with me.

I don't know how many days that I'll live,
Or what the future has to hold.
But I do know this, dearest Pamela,
It's with you that I want to grow old.

~Richmond, BC - July 2020

CONTENTS

Poetry

Flash Fiction

A Life Well Lived

Holding his grandson's hand, an old gentleman was shuffling along on an English Bay sidewalk and sat on a bench to rest. He was tired.

"Come on, grandpa, let's keep going," the little four-year-old said as he pulled on his grandfather's hand.

"No, I have to rest for a few moments," the old man responded. "But here, I've brought some colored chalk for you. Why don't you draw a picture for me?"

He reached into his pocket and gave the chalk to his grandson. Placated, the child accepted the chalk with glee. "What should I draw, Grandpa?" he asked.

"Whatever you wish," was his response, "surprise me."

While the child squatted on the sidewalk, the old gentleman watched his grandson with pride and joy. He fondly remembered the time when he had walked his youngest daughter down the aisle to marry her future husband and the elation of the birth of his grandson.

As the fall's sun streamed down to warm him, a kaleidoscope of memory images flashed through his mind while he reminisced about how his life had evolved. He concluded that he had no regrets.

While listening to the occasional cooing of nearby pigeons, he watched his grandson drawing a rainbow in front of him. It seemed to him that the child, even at his young age, had instinctively captured a symbol of hope that he drew on the sidewalk. He smiled and was pleased.

He had pulled the brim of his fedora down a bit lower to shield his eyes from the sun. While he watched his grandson drawing, his eyelids drooped one last time as he fell asleep.

After his grandson finished his picture, and asked, "How do you like it, Grandpa?"

Because there was no answer, the little boy tugged on his grandfather's hand. Still, there was no response. The little boy didn't understand why. He kept tugging his grandfather's hand as he cried, "Come on, Grandpa. Wake up. I want to go home. I have to go pee."

A lady strolled by as the little boy began to cry and asked what was wrong. Hearing the child's lament, she realized that his grandfather would never respond. She called emergency services on her cell to look after the old gentleman. Meanwhile, she consoled the child and was able to find an address to take the little boy home.

First Love

After some passionate kisses, Liz was resting her head on Dave's chest as he held her close. It was a lovely, warm summer evening. He had found a little-known trail that he was able to navigate in his VW Beatle to a parking spot.

"Do you believe in the Bible?' he asked out of the blue.

"Why are you asking me that?" she laughed, "of course I do. I go to Mass every Sunday. Why do you want to know?"

"Well," he continued, "Apparently, we're supposed to have twelve ribs on each side of our rib cages. But what I don't understand is that, according to the Scriptures, God apparently created Eve from one of Adam's ribs. So technically, I should only have eleven on one side or the other. Yet it appears that I have twelve on each side."

"Here, you can count them yourself," he said as he raised his left arm.

Liz felt around, above his belt under his unbuttoned shirt, for a moment to find his first and lowest rib. Then she started to let her fingers climb up each rib, like climbing a stair, to the top rib. She could feel his heart beating and couldn't resist tickling his breast as she continued to the top.

"Yup, you definitely got twelve ribs," she giggled as she concluded her exploration. "Maybe women have one less rib. I don't know. I've never wondered about that."

"Do you want to find out?" he asked.

"Sure. Why not?"

She turned to face him and raised her arms. David started to let the fingers of his right hand start to press in on her blouse as he counted off her ribs. However, when he got to her fifth rib, he encountered the obstruction of her bra.

"Well, that takes care of that," he said. "I can't go any further."

"Oh, you're being silly," she responded as she unbuttoned her blouse, unsnapped her brassier, removed the items, and threw them onto the rear seat. "There, now you can count them."

David was flabbergasted. He had not expected this from her. Liz was the first girl with whom he was truly in love. Furthermore, he was a neophyte when it came to any sexual encounter. However, he became aroused when he saw the beautiful orbs of her bare breasts and the pink nipples.

Somewhat flustered, he started his counting again and was able to get to her sixth and seventh ribs with no problems. However, on impulse, he allowed his hand to move over to the top of her left breast and stroke it. Gently, he squeezed her nipple between his finger and thumb. As it stiffened, he pulled her close and moved his head down to suckle it. Carefully, so as not to hurt her, he gently let his lips and tongue massage it as if he were caressing a peeled grape. Liz moaned as she twisted her body and pressed her breast more into his face.

"Oh my God," she cried in ecstasy, "don't stop! Please don't stop."

She reached down to his crotch and found that his manhood had hardened. She stroked it. In a blur of activity, they undressed each other. He slid over into the passenger seat while she straddled him and guided his stiff shaft inside her.

While they copulated, they shared more passionate kisses that seemed to last forever during their intercourse. Being the first time for him, he only lasted for a few seconds before his release.

They remained coupled until nature decreed that his flaccid manhood could no longer defy the contractions of her vaginal muscles and was expelled. He had hoped to remain inside her forever, but it was not to be. Yet they continued to kiss passionately on the lips and on each other's breasts for a while longer. Very little was spoken between moans as they explored each other's bodies with ecstasy. Exhausted, they finally ceased and got dressed.

Once dressed, they were again ensconced in each other's arms. A full moon had risen and was shining down at them as they shared more kisses.

"That was great," Dave remarked in a soft voice, "but you know, I never did find out whether you have eleven or twelve ribs."

"Well," she chuckled, "I guess that maybe you'll just have to find that out next time."

Her Mistake

Just after shutting her suite's door, pressing the padlock icon on her automatic door lock, and hearing the bolt lazily sliding home, she realized her mistake. Immediately, she keyed in her four-digit access code, but the lock would not respond.

Her mistake was that she had left her door key on the umbrella stand in the hall when she pulled on her boots. She should have known better. After all, the replace light on the inside had been flashing red for several weeks, indicating dying batteries.

Now they were dead, and now she had to find a locksmith.

Chrome Dome

Right after graduation, Jerry enlisted in the Air Force and became a pilot, flying primarily F18s. In one of his training flights, his jet developed mechanical problems, and he had to eject. Although he survived the crash, unfortunately, the doctors had to do some major surgery and reconstruction of his face and skull. But, modern medical prowess being what it is, no one ever knew how much metal had been used to put his head and face back together except, of course, the security gates at various airports.

He would warn the security officer that the alarm would be triggered when he walked through the metal detector. As the detectors became more sensitive, it was becoming a bit of a hassle having to explain him constantly. He finally got a document and card from the federal government, which gave him a search exemption when he triggered the alarm.

In the mid1990, in spite of his previous injuries, he decided to fight Sadaam Hussein on the American's side during the first Dessert Storm initiative by George Bush. His dad had been an American and a fighter pilot, while his mother was French-Canadian. And although he was Canadian, he had decided that this was what he wanted to do.

Outside of Kirkuk, his plane was shot down, but he parachuted safely to the ground. Unfortunately, upon landing, he badly sprained his ankle. He was taken prisoner by some local militia and incarcerated. He knew, however, that his unit would be looking for him soon because he had sent out an SOS before he went down, plus he had a homing device sewn into his apparel.

One of his captors was a sadist who liked to mete out certain tortures to Americans for the merriment of his associates. Jerry was subjected to various body blows from fists, sticks, and rifle stocks.

During one of these, his scalp was lacerated badly, and he was bleeding profusely, which seemed to arouse more punishment.

Although he could not properly stand on his injured ankle, the torture numbed much of his pain. His sadistic captor taunted him and came at him. He was able to feign a body injury, and as his antagonist rushed forward, Jerry was able to kick him in the groin with his injured foot, dropping his captor. As the guy got up, Jerry's head-butted the Iraqi and split the guy's forehead above one eye.

As a result of the pummeling that he had received from rifle butts and head butting his adversary, Jerry's titanium skull plate shifted slightly, and a metallic spur stuck out of his forehead. He went at his opponent again and raked the spur across the other's face, leaving a deep gash and destroying one eye. Screams of pain and insults ensued.

It's not certain whether it was the screams or the homing device that had his comrades break into the compound and rescue him just in the nick of time.

He was flown to Germany to an army hospital, had his ankle set and immobilized to heal, and had his skull plate refitted. The only problem, he was advised, was that half of his scalp had been torn off and that it would take at least six to eight months for it to grow back.

"What?" he remarked with some chagrin, "I'm going to be a chrome dome that long? Hell, how can I make time with some of these gorgeous nurses?"

"Oh, don't worry, Liebchen," a female voice from behind him said, "I'm sure we'll find a way."

And with that, a curvaceous young nurse came into view and continued, "I really love you, fly boys."

Disbelief

Allyson was a straight "A" student in Grade 10 and a high school cheerleader. She had heard from one of her girlfriends that the school's hunk had a new speedboat, which was tied up at the jetty by the river. Being curious, she wanted to see it.

As she leaned over the railing, she adjusted her schoolbag in a bandolier style over her shoulder so that it wouldn't shift as she climbed down the wooden ladder to a lower-level platform. Her boot, however, slipped on one of the rungs, and she was thrown into the stream.

She had never liked swimming and only knew how to dog paddle. The only reason that she ever went to a beach was to be able to wear a bikini to show off her body for boys and men to ogle and to get a tan. She had not expected to be floating downstream in frigid mid-April water.

She tried to paddle to shore, but her waterlogged coat and water-filled sheepskin boots were dragging her down. Then she remembered someone telling her about the lamprey eels that were in this river. She panicked and wildly flailed her arms. Although she struggled to swim to shore, she was drawn into the stream's current.

Physically weakened and with hypothermia setting in, her thinking was inhibited, and she did not think to jettison the items dragging her down. Her sporadic splashing became anemic and futile.

She was found about a couple of miles downstream, where her schoolbag was snagged on a sunken tree branch. Her eyes and mouth were wide open as if in disbelief.

Abortion

"Mom," the little five-year-old said, "I need to ask you something," and opened the door to his mother's bedroom. Bewildered, all that he saw was his mother in a fetal position, barely covered under a bloodied sheet.

"Quick," she whispered hoarsely, "go get grandma."

With legs pumping, in tears, the boy ran to the house two doors down, crying, "Oma, Oma."

His grandmother stopped her sewing as he appeared. "What is it, my child?"

"Mom needs you; she's bleeding!" he replied. In his shock, he had not seen the knitting needles on his mother's bed nor the bloodied bucket with an aborted fetus by the bedside.

The old lady got there just in time to stanch her daughter's hemorrhaging, and while one life was lost, another was saved. This was the age before the pill when poor women went to desperate measures to stop having to feed another mouth.

It's such a gruesome topic, hard to comprehend.

"How can you even talk about this?" they asked later.

"'Cause," he replied, "she was my mom."

The Junkie

He was scrunched up in a doorway on Powell Street, shivering. His threadbare shirt couldn't protect him from the February cold, and even if it could, it couldn't stop his shivering from withdrawal symptoms. He had not had a hit in the last eight hours and was anxiously waiting for his dealer to show up.

Meanwhile, his older sister was combing all his usual haunts in the Downtown Eastside to find him. A former drug addict herself, she had gone through various rehabilitation programs and been clean for almost three years. And she had a job. Now, she wanted to help her younger sibling to do the same.

They had briefly spoken the previous day and were to get together for lunch earlier at a greasy spoon on East Hastings, but he was a 'no show.' So she started to check out various places and spoke with some of the people who she still knew and who also knew her brother.

His teeth chattered from the cold, and his need for more drugs didn't help. A shadow in a hoodie appeared which Sam recognized. It was his savior, his drug connection.

"Geesh, man," he chattered, "glad to see ya. I need a fix badly."

The dealer was unemotional; he had seen many of his clients in this state before.

"I've got some stuff here, but it's gonna cost you a C-note," he said.

"Shit," cried Sam, "that's double what ya charged before. All I got is fifty bucks."

"Take it or leave it," came the response.

Sam started to cry, adding to his shivers. He pleaded with his dealer, sobbing, "Puleeze." He continued, "Look, I stole a Rolex off some drunk. I'll give it to you an' all the money I got. Please, I gotta have my fix!"

Curious, the dealer said, "Show me."

Sam reached into his pocket and extracted the watch. It looked like a Rolex, but the dealer knew that it was a fake. Nevertheless, he could hawk it, and the money would easily cover his costs. Besides, he had just received a new batch of fentanyl-laden pills that he wanted to slough off. He kept the watch.

"All right, give me the money, and I'll give you the stuff." And with that, the exchange was made.

Sam was too cold to crush and liquefy the drug to be able to inject it. Instead, he swallowed almost the entire package of pills that he had just bought. It took a little time for the ingested drugs to hit his system, but when they did, he no longer felt the cold.

While he floated in and out of consciousness, he had a hallucination that someone else was standing there and talking to him. Trying to stay conscious and open his eyes, he couldn't make out the person. However, he recognized the voice as that of his sister, who had finally found her young brother.

The last thing that he felt before permanent darkness overcame him, was the warmth of a jacket draped around him and being cradled in his sister's arms on the sidewalk.

The Challenge

"Years ago, when I was in my late twenties, a number of guys with whom I used to hang around used to love to challenge me. They would taunt me by saying that, 'You know you can't do that.' Being quite self-confident in my abilities to the point of arrogance, they knew that I was up for almost any challenge," he said as he took a sip of his brandy. Then he continued and told me his story.

"One weekend, four of us were staying overnight in an old hunting camp. Since it was not yet hunting season, we imbibed a lot of beer and other mind-altering ingredients. With inhibitions being lowered and emboldened, each tried to impress the others with our individual prowess in various tests such as arm wrestles, leg wrestles, and, finally, just denigrating into regular body wrestling.

One other challenge was target shooting with various rifles and a couple of pistols. Although pistols were restricted guns, one of the guys was an off-duty RCMP officer who had a federal permit to possess and shoot them. He proved to be a crack shot with each. Although I had been a marksman in the army reserves, I was bested by him in rifle shooting.

Then he brought out a S&W .44 Magnum revolver, the same model that Clint Eastwood used as Dirty Harry in his movies. Although it shows Dirty Harry shooting the revolver using only one hand in his movies, the cop said that it was virtually impossible to do so. He claimed that two hands were required to shoot this pistol and to have a proper stance. He claimed that the movies had taken license by showing one-hand shooting. This sounded like a challenge to me.

'I'll bet that I can shoot the revolver with one hand,' I said with some bravado. Brandy had loosened my tongue.

Of course, I had dropped the gauntlet. I was immediately told that I would not be able to shoot single-handed. Emboldened by some derision, I further embellished the challenge by saying that I would fire all six rounds in less than half a minute. 'You're fuckin' nuts!' I was told.

I picked up the Model 29. With its 6 1/2" barrel, it was relatively heavy. However, I figured that this would be a bit of an advantage because the weight would minimize the recoil. However, I didn't know what to expect as I took the revolver and faced the target.

Having previously aimed other pistols at targets fifty feet away, I felt that aiming would be, more or less, instinctive. Wrong. I held the revolved straight ahead while aiming it at the target like I would normally and squeezed the trigger. Holy Shit, my hand went straight up while my arm moved back and almost spun me around. Meanwhile, tingling started in my wrist.

I heard several snickers. 'Ya were told ya can't shoot the thing single-handed.'

Being pissed off now, I turned very slightly so that my right arm could easily absorb any recoil without hitting my torso and allowed a free upward motion from the recoil. Having been vexed by the comments, I rapidly fired the remaining five rounds. My arm went back to cushion the recoil, and my hand went up as well after each round. Although I hit the target, the shots were somewhat wild.

When done, I laid the revolver on the bench. 'You're a crazy son of a bitch,' someone remarked, 'you're nuts.'

'No,' I responded, 'I just knew that I could do this,' while gritting my teeth at the creeping pain in my wrist.

What I never told anyone was that my wrist hurt for about three days afterward, and I had no feeling in my hand to speak of as well. Yet it had been worth it just to prove a point. But also, I never fired a big-bore pistol ever again with only one hand."

New Dress

Wearing her pretty new pink dress and shiny new black sandals, the little girl strutted past a young couple to a riverbank abutment at the back of her property, followed by her exuberant Samoyed pup. She passed and ignored a young couple making out on a beach blanket, and they ignored her.

She and her family had picnicked there the previous weekend. Her older brother had shown her how to twirl daisies between his thumb and forefinger so that they looked like helicopters gently floating onto the water.

As she tried to emulate her brother's twirling technique, she became frustrated that she could not get her daisy blossoms to twirl. Meanwhile, her dog was barking and running around, causing discomfort to the young couple whose intimacy had been disrupted.

As they started to fold up their blanket, they heard a splash. Looking around, the little girl was not in sight, but the dog was barking furiously at the water. It took them a few seconds to realize that the child had fallen into the river.

Eyes wide open and instinctively holding her breath, the girl felt herself sinking and floating downstream with the river current. For a fraction of a second, she remembered her mom's admonition not to mess up her new dress. She peed herself. As she started to let out her breath, a hand grabbed her, and she was propelled into daylight and air.

The young fellow from the blanket had jumped into the river and rescued her.

Laid on the unfurled blanket, she gasped for air. Fortunately, she had not inhaled any water.

Frightened, she started to cry and got up. She did not want any help or condolence from the young couple. Instead, she just wanted to run home to her mother, although she was afraid of what her mom would do and say about the dress.

She was too young, however, to realize that her life would be more precious to her mother than any soaked new dress.

Leeches

Apparently there are somewhere around 700 different varieties of leeches in the world. Most of these bloodsuckers live primarily in fresh water.

Near Tommy's house, there was a creek that had leeches. Although this seven-year-old kid didn't really like to handle them, his dad showed him how to avoid getting stuck with one on his body while catching some with a slotted spoon or stick. They made great bait for fishing trout, almost better than worms. The lad wanted to surprise his dad by catching some leeches so that they could go fishing together.

While he was bent over at the creek's bridge and had about ten or twelve leeches in his jar, a scraggly vagrant had sneaked up behind him and grabbed Tommy by the genitals.

"Ow," he screamed, "don't do that," and scrabbled away.

"Com mere, little one," the vagrant growled with a toothless smile, "we're gonna have us some fun."

"No, I don't want to."

Tommy was both scared yet somewhat unafraid. His dad had taught his son some defensive and evasive moves, which kicked in. As the thirty-something guy approached him, Tommy grabbed his jar of leeches and threw them in the vagrant's face.

As he ran home as fast as he could, the last thing Tommy remembered was the pervert, screaming and swearing, swatting at his face and neck as some of the leeches slid down his chest under his shirt.

Failing Memory

After a couple of hours, on a trip to his Toronto's head office, his eyes became strained. Soon, the report he was reading faded into a blur of lines as his eyes glazed over. He tried to focus on the text but was unable to concentrate. He was tired; he had gotten up at five a.m. to catch his flight.

Resting his receding hairline, or as he preferred to call it, his "high forehead," against the coolness of the plane's molded window side panel, he looked out across the vastness below him from six-plus miles in the air. Blotches of dark green, probably wooded areas, were interspersed in a checkerboard of light brown, yellow, dark brown, and more green fields below. It looked like a patchwork quilt.

He wondered how big the fields actually were. Were they a section? Half a section? Quarter section? And how big is a section anyway? He didn't know. It was just a term that he had heard from some friends living in Alberta.

Some roads zigzagged in a north-south direction, while others ran east to west. He recalled talking to an acquaintance who had driven from Toronto to Calgary one time, some 2,200 miles, in a couple of days. Once he had hit Winnipeg, he said that he could have put his car on automatic pilot had he had one. A straight line across Manitoba and Saskatchewan, as far as Alberta's foothills. Nothing but flat terrain. Total boredom.

His eyes wandered across the flat land mass onto the clouds, hanging like fluffs of cotton below. In the distance, he could see a massive accumulation of them. "Cumulous?" he wondered, "or cumulonimbus?" He tried to recall his grade eight science course where they had taught about these things. All he could recall was that cumulonimbus clouds were a thundercloud formation with an anvil-shaped top. These were definitely not thunderclouds. "Damn, wish I could recall what they are."

The fact that he could not remember what the various cloud formations were annoyed him. Someone had once said that education is all that one remembers after one has forgotten all the stuff one has learned. True, but stupid. "They're probably cumulous," he finally resolved.

A thin, brownish layer below caught his attention. Smog. Goddamn pollution. "Where are we?" he wondered. The announcement ten minutes ago said that Swift Current was on the left and Montana was on the right. Brandon? He could not remember his geography. "What industry in Brandon would cause such smog? We're probably closer to Winnipeg," he thought. He knew that there were smoke-belching industries there.

"Shit, I must be getting old. Can't remember simple geography," he thought. Reaching for Skyword, he tried to determine where they might be from the airline's route map. It was futile. He replaced the magazine in the seat pocket.

Finally, being tired, his eyelids drooped, and he dozed off to sleep.

A Father's Advice

We had just graduated from junior high school and were looking forward to a summer reprieve before entering our senior high school classes next semester in September. Gail was my bestie; we could always tell each other our innermost secrets. While she went to Newcastle to spend some time with her grandparents for the break, I flew west to visit my dad in BC for a couple of weeks.

The flight was uneventful. He was there to greet me at the airport and to take me home. For a few days, my father and my stepmom fussed over me. Then, one weekend, we drove from Vancouver to Sheridan Lake to visit one of my dad's friends, who lived in a modernized rustic log cabin near the lake. We enjoyed a few carefree days in conviviality with lots of swimming, canoeing, and bar-b-ques.

One day, before leaving, my dad asked me if I wanted to go for a spin in a 4x4, which his friend owned because he was looking to buy a similar vehicle. I had always enjoyed my dad's off-road exploits, so I readily agreed.

After grabbing a few beers, we went down some old logging roads and backwoods trails while he checked out the vehicle's four-wheel drive capabilities. At one point, he said to me, "By the way, one reason that I asked you along is to have a heart-to-heart chat with you."

"Oh Dad," I said, "If we're going to talk about the birds and the bees, Mom and I have already had that conversation."

"No," he responded, "I'm going to tell you how the guys are going to try to charm their way into your panties and all the tricks that they'll use. I know because I've tried every one of them!"

And with that, he proceeded to tell me about the excuses and lies that I was likely to hear from any guy who wanted to have sex with me.

He talked about how a guy would try to make me feel sorry for him because he needed me so badly that it hurt and he couldn't sleep. Or, if I didn't do it, he would jump off a bridge.

Dad told me that if any guy used any of those and other ploys, to just tell him to either masturbate or that I would help him find an appropriate bridge and that I should help him to jump off it. In either case, he said, get rid of the idiot.

"And remember," he continued, "Always squeeze a quarter between your knees so that when you go out on a date, and you refuse to have sex with the guy, he'll likely dump you and leave you stranded out of revenge. At least you'll always have money for a pay phone to call your mom to pick you up."

"But as you get older," he continued, "there'll come a time when you'll get some overwhelming feelings where you want to make love when making out with a guy. There is nothing wrong with wanting to cuddle up to someone and have sex. It is a beautiful act."

"Just make sure that the man who takes your virginity is worthy of your gift because it is yours to give, not his to take. Also, make sure that you're on the pill because the odds are that he won't be using a condom," he concluded.

Finally, after about an hour of driving and regaling on about sex to me, we had returned to the cabin. All I could do was reach over and give him a big hug and kiss because the advice that he had given me was something my mom had never done. She is a bit of a prude, whereas my dad was a realist and more broad-minded. Even though I was his "little girl", he treated me like an adult; hence, he allowed me to have a beer.

While Gail, a couple of other girlfriends, and I had talked about boys and fantasized about sex, none of us had done it or had admitted to having done it. Aside from the fear of pregnancy, I was not interested in the least at the time to have any relationship with any guy, platonic or otherwise.

Years later, I talked to my older brother over a couple of drinks after meeting my future husband, and we chatted about our dad. We finally got onto the subject of our sexual activity as teens. He chuckled as he told me about a chat that our dad had with my brother, somewhat similar to what dad had told me, which really surprised me.

The major difference appeared to have been that, although dad had told my bother much of the same mantra, except, as my brother explained, our father told my brother that if he ever knocked up some young woman, father expected my brother to do the appropriate thing. Either my brother had to marry the girl, or if an abortion was required, he would pay for what he had done.

And here I had always thought that Dad was putting all the pressure on me to be a good daughter because I was the vulnerable one who could get pregnant! Yet he also gave my brother his expectations and marching orders to do the right thing.

It's funny, though, as I sit here as a single mom on what's supposed to be my fifteenth wedding anniversary, I still think about my dad's advice and think that I should have that talk with my thirteen-year-old daughter. Her father couldn't care less after he abandoned us years ago.

The Bet

Turned off by the melodramatic schmaltz on their television, his macho self exclaimed, "This is stupid, making the guy feel elated and pissed off at the same time. That would never work on me!"

"Wanna bet?" his wife asked.

"I'll bet you $100 dollars that it won't!"

"Okay," she said, "of all your red neck buddies, I think that you're still the best one in the sack."

Encounter with A Lynx

For about an hour or so, I had been sitting on a log overlooking a meadow keeping an eye out for a moose. Still early in the season, daytime temperatures had been reaching $24^0 C$., so I was not too optimistic that one would walk out. And since we had not yet seen any cows, we figured that the bulls were more than likely still up Green Mountain. Besides, it was only around 5:30 pm with legal dark still a couple of hours away. But, one never knew, one could get lucky.

Since it had sprinkled a bit of liquid sunshine earlier as I had arrived at my hunting spot, I decided to make a crude structure over which I could pull a tarp or poncho as a bivouac to stay out of the rain. However, once completed, it proved unnecessary since the sprinkles had stopped.

So there I sat, a bit bored. While reminiscing about some previous hunts and successes in this area, the incessant chatter of a squirrel had started to get on my nerves.

I know that the calls, which squirrels and crows make, are often beacons to alert various forest denizens of intruders, and I believe that is what had happened here.

As the squirrel continued to make its unrelenting and irritating noise, I had got up from the log to stretch my legs and to see where the pesky rodent was located. However, as I rotated 180 degree, I was startled by the appearance of a lynx not more that twelve feet away on a parallel log behind the one on which I had been seated.

It stood still and didn't move. What a gorgeous animal! It was the size of a German shepherd dog, probably about fifty pounds. The tuffs on its ears were at least two inches long. It was displaying its winter coat because the legs were about a couple of inches across, and its paws were the size of the palm of my hand. My eyes met its tawny gaze.

Although I had both my loaded rifle and a bear spray canister at arm's length away, I didn't move to retrieve either. Instead, I threw up my hands and growled "aarrgh" in as a menacing way as possible. The lynx just stood there and looked at me as if to say, "So who are you trying to impress?" I don't think that this animal had ever seen a human close up.

After about fifteen or twenty seconds, it slid off the log and slowly started to pad away. Its pace was unhurried. The thought of shooting or pepper spaying it had momentarily crossed my mind. It had been a perfect target for either action. However, being a meat hunter, I don't believe in killing an animal just for the sake of killing it, nor did I believe that I had to put it into pain with bear spray since I was not being attacked.

I watched this magnificent animal retreat into its wilderness domain with the slow and graceful moves of the wild cat that it was. Unfortunately my camera had been buried in my back pack, so I did not get a picture. But, as I reminisce about this encounter, I am absolutely both humbled and thrilled to have had this experience.

Now had this been a cougar . . .

Goulash Story

Way back in the early 70s, my older sister Margaret and her family lived in Brewster, NY.

I had driven down to Brewster in a borrowed pick-up truck with my son Sheldon, who would have been about five at the time, to haul back a DKW 4x4. This was one of only 2,000 vehicles manufactured for the German army as a prototype by Auto Union, which became a division of Volkswagen. Later, these vehicles were re-engineered by VW to become the Iltis and then sold off to Bombardier to become our Canadian army's answer to Jeep.

When I got it back to New Brunswick, I had the only "Deek" in captivity east of Montreal. It had a 3-cylinder, water-cooled, two-stroke engine with a governor on the throttle. It was the same engine that Saab used in their early sedans - they were tanks! Fortunately, I also received an extra set of pistons from my mechanic brother-in-law, each of which was different from the others because of their porting.

Once I got back to NB, I had to try my new toy out, of course. In trying to traverse a rather steep hill and flooring the gas pedal, the engine suddenly started to inexplicably not accelerate any faster, scaring the hell out of me. I had expected to use revs to overcome the obstacle, but this beast was not responding as expected. In checking under the hood, I noticed the centrifugally operated governor, which backed the gas pedal off above a certain number of revs.

Heck, you can't have something like this interfere with fun now, can you!? So I disconnected the linkage, much to my chagrin.

It was not long afterwards that I over revved the engine and blew one of the pistons.A mechanic friend and I tore the engine down and had to replace all three pistons because the other two were also on their last legs.What a job! We got the thing back together and reattached the governor.It was a lesson learned.

But I digress …

While at Margaret's home, she served a dish of goulash that was different from the way our mother used to make it. It was simply delicious! Among various ingredients, she had something in it that I thought were sliced kidneys.

When I called her one time for a family chat, I mentioned to her that I had made her Goulash but found that the kidneys were a little strong and should be parboiled a bit first. She asked, "What kidneys?" I told her what we had in Brewster, upon which she laughed and told me that the items I mistook for kidneys were sliced mushrooms.

Another lesson learned.

Fire Lighting Contest

When I was about 12 years old, I wandered off one June Saturday to Rockwood Park in Saint John. Lilly Lake, a popular swimming hole for us locals, was one of the main attractions in the park.

It was still a tad too cold to take a dip. However, a local Gyro club had organized some activities for kids around my age.

There were various athletic contests like running, broad jump, high jump, tug-a-war, and others. Most of these had left me disinterested because the only running that I really enjoyed, namely cross country, was not on the agenda.

One scheduled activity, however, caught my attention. They had set up eight stations on a sandy stretch of beach for a fire lighting contest. Each station had three pieces of 1 x 2's about 15" long and two old-fashioned self-strike kitchen matches lying next to the spot where the fire was to be built. Then, there were metal rods with a hook on the end embedded into the sand on an angle. And a tin, filled half full of water, was suspended from each rod above the fire pit.

I had had a fascination with fires for quite some time. When my family immigrated to Canada, my English vocabulary consisted of about 20 words. Hence, I occupied myself in the nearby woods by building a lean-to with a fire pit, which I frequently used. Then, every spring, burning the dry grasses of a field across the street from my house was always a treat because I was allowed to spread the fire to little patches of unburned weeds.

These grass fires were usually under the control of the farmer who owned the field. However, occasionally, the dry field would mysteriously catch fire earlier in the spring. It's amazing how a short candle, nestled amongst some dry grass and shielded from the wind by an inverted flower pot, could light wax-soaked dry tinder as the candle burned down to its end. And, of course, there was no one ever around who could be identified as the pyromaniac!

So when they announced a fire lighting contest, I was one the first kids to sign up.

An old pocket knife that I had with me had a broken tip, and it did not have the sharpest blades. Once the contest started, each kid started to whittle shavings from their pieces of wood. But because of my dull knife, I struggled to carve shavings quickly, which was noticed by a wizen spectator.

"Here," the old gentleman said as he handed me an opened folding knife. It was razor sharp, which scared the heck out of me. However, once the blade bit into the wood, I was surprised how I was able to control the blade and whittle shavings with ease. My kindling pile started to grow rapidly.

While I was still making shavings, a couple of the boys had lit their piles. Boy, was I tempted to do likewise, but the old gent told me to wait and keep whittling. By the time I got to my last piece of wood, I had quite a pile of shavings. Meanwhile, half of the boys had already started their fires with their dads cheering them on. I desperately wanted to do the same but I kept on cutting.

Finally, I had a huge pile of kindling, most of which I carefully heaped under my Billie pot. As one of the last ones to do so, I struck one match and lit the tinder. Within seconds, I had a roaring fire going. Meanwhile, most of the guys who had started their fires earlier had to coax tiny flames back to life to heat their pots while they started making more shavings.

My fire quickly became the largest by far as I carefully fed it more shavings from my remaining pile. Within minutes, my pot began to boil. And it was the first to do so! As the water boiled, foam rose to the top, overflowing the pot and onto my fire, which killed it. Interestingly, the organizers had put a detergent into the water in each pot. My fire was the first to be doused hence, I won the contest.

The prize was a two-spool, 6-pound Stren monofilament fishing line. Up to that point, my fishing lines had always consisted of some heavy-duty sewing thread that my mother had given me for my homemade fishing rod. This twelve-year-old couldn't have been prouder to get some real fishing line at last!

I found the old gentleman to return his knife and to thank to him. He told me that, "If you're going to have a knife on you, son, it should always be sharp. Otherwise, a dull knife is virtually useless and can be very dangerous."

It was advice that I've heeded ever since. Over the years, I learned how to sharpen knives, and all the various knives that I use in the kitchen or for hunting have an edge sharp enough on them with which I can shave.

Later that afternoon, free hotdogs and ice cream were served. After having had my fill, I headed for home as one very happy camper.

My Last Deer Hunt

September 26th is Shirley's birthday. Most years, Neil would miss her birthday because he was away hunting. And since he had died, I decided to drive up to Cherryville to either take my favorite Okanagan Lady out for a birthday dinner or I would cook dinner for her. It was her choice. She opted for the latter.

Of course, deer season was also open. It was reported that very few bucks had been seen in the fields, but lots of does. This could have been as a result of the abnormally dry summer and/or the fact that the property across the south end of the ranch was being actively logged. Lots of times, years ago, we would see upwards of 50 deer in the bottom fields. The evening that I arrived, I briefly sat in a blind and counted at least 17 or 18 does and fawns. But no bucks.

Wednesday morning, I went to the Cherryville gun range to do some target shooting with various rifles and pistols that I had brought with me. My hunting rifle was sighted in for 200 yards, so it shot about 2 – 3 inches high of bull's eye at my 100-yard target. After a couple of hours of plinking and shooting fun, I left the range and headed back to the ranch.

That evening, I decided to sit in a different blind. As I was watching the lengthening shadow of the blind ooze out in front of me around 6:20, a two-point buck sauntered out of a copse of poplar and fir trees. He was about 90 to 100 yards away. Because I did not want to hit the whitetail where it could ruin a lot of meat, I aimed for the neck and squeezed the trigger. I missed.

The buck ran back into the trees but came right back out and trotted off to my left. He then angled towards my blind. I did not have a very clear view of him because of some branches in front of the blind's window opening, so I had to extend the barrel of my rifle out of the opening. This movement caught the eye of the buck, and he stopped about 75 yards away. As he turned slightly, ready to bolt, I aimed at the lower part of his body, just behind the front leg and into the lung area. I heard the "smuck" as the bullet hit and brought the deer down.

Because it was on the other side of a fence from where I was, I drove my vehicle across the field that I was in and up to the house. There, I grabbed a side-by-side quad and, in a couple of minutes, drove it into the field where the buck lay.

The deer was too heavy for me to heave it into the box of the quad, so I hauled it head-first onto the vehicle floor on the passenger side. Hanging onto a hind leg so that the deer wouldn't slide out, I then proceeded to the area where a block and tackle had been set up. As I started to skin out one of the hind legs to get rid of the scent gland, it became obvious that I needed to hang the carcass from a gambrel iron to make the job easier.

Unfortunately, due to the lack of length of rope, the gambrel could not be lowered sufficiently for me to hook it into the leg that I had already started to skin out. Also, since I had a recent back injury, I could not lift the deer sufficiently high enough. So I called Shirley, who came down to where I was and helped me load the carcass into my vehicle. I had already called our local butcher to dress out the deer and to skin it.

In less than two hours, the deer was hanging in a cooler, ready for further processing. Gutted, but with the skin still on, the buck weighed 104 lbs. There was some tasty noshing from that animal.

This episode, however, also made me realize that without Neil, hunting would never be the same. And I questioned myself if it was really that important to me. I felt that I knew enough guys with whom I'd shared venison in the past, and surely I could talk one of them out of some stew meat or ground.

Hence, I sold several of my toys that go "bang," including my favorite hunting rifle. It was a bit traumatic for me to divest myself of my Remington 7mm Mauser. But at least I have some great memories of using it with the reloads that Neil and I used to make while quaffing a glass of red or brandy.

If I Could Add a Day

If I could add a day to any month, I would want it in mid-September so as to observe and experience the scents and colors of autumn, especially the scarlet of mountain sumacs and sugar maples, as well as green pine trees with gnarly cones that are falling to the ground, and tall, slim, golden aspens, framed by a cloudless cerulean sky.

Cool fall zephyrs would blow through my receding hairline while bringing the fresh scent of sweet grass to the breeze and creating ripples on the lake. I'd navigate my canoe to the other shore with gentle paddle strokes.

Poetry

Open & Free & Rhyming Verse

While Picasso painted pictures with paints,
I prefer to paint my pictures with words.
Finding the right words to express my thoughts
Can, however, be arduous at times.
Free verse and open verse are some formats,
And iambic pentameter and rhymes
May add lyrical sounds to the scribbles.

Or perhaps not!

for example, where is it written that a verse must rhyme
except perhaps in my own mind
and that it must conform to a certain number of lines and with
strict formatting
or require a set number of syllables
allow no caps or commas or periods or punctuation of any kind
nay, it is not written thus
so just leave it all to the reader's imagination to fill in the
missing details

But I might also write in rhyming couplets like:

With all that having been said,
Yet I also have a dread,
That unrhymed words I must axe.
'Cause I love rhyming syntax.

Or maybe I'll choose to rhyme alternate lines:

With all that having been said,
I love all rhyming syntax,
But I also have a dread,
That unrhymed lines I must axe.

The Mason

A piercing cry of fear was heard,
As the mason began to fall
From his ethereal workstation,
High up on the cathedral wall.

All stopped and stared in disbelief
In horror and in awe, as he
Tumbled safely down to the ground
- His fall broken by an old tree.

He picked himself up, unshaken.
By what had just occurred to him.
In the nearest tavern, his luck
He toasted long with beer and gin.

Vanity, oh fool, led him on,
As boisterously he would tell,
"The grim Reaper, I have cheated;
He missed as he rang my bell!"

Thus on and on throughout the night,
Of fate, he made a mockery.
Never once thinking to thank God,
And to get down on bended knee.

Sleep overcame the rowdy guest,
As at last, he made way to bed.
On the stairs, he stumbled and fell,
They found him there next morning – dead.

Perhaps if he had gone straight home
To the arms of his loving wife,
Given thanks, 'stead of blasphemy,
The mason might still be alive.

The fix

Between the town's peep show
and the adult bookstore,
there is a coffee shop
where one can get a score.

The jukebox is playing
a mournful country song,
swaying to its rhythm,
a druggie sings along.

So, while Kristofferson sings
about a lonely morn
and a sleepy sidewalk,
the junkie feels forlorn.

Demons in his veins are
demanding to be fed;
he craves another hit
before he goes to bed.

His connection appears,
just in the nick of time,
to satisfy his need
and make him feel sublime.

'Stead of getting cocaine,
it's fentanyl instead;
his fix is poisonous,
by morning, he'll be dead.

Winter Morning

Walking up the path under an azure sky,
I crunched the snow beneath my feet.
Paperwhite birches, heavily crusted with ice,
bowed to the earth.
The sun's rays scintillated through the icy branches as if
through a thousand diamonds.
Stopping to sniff the cold, clear morning air, I marveled at
what my senses perceived.
I felt the presence of God and was at peace with the world.

One Soul More

While a city slept,
The death knell sounded.
And up from hell's fires,
The devil bounded.
On cloven hooves,
Across the roofs,
With gleaming eyes,
His prey he spies.
        One Soul More.

Alberta Foothills

Out in Alberta's foothills
under a silver autumn moon,
A campfire was burning while
a cowboy was humming a tune.

In his mind, he was dancing
with the fair girl of his dreams,
A girl he had left behind –
his angel in faded blue jeans.

He looked up into the sky
with no clouds; the night was clear.
A gentle breeze was blowing,
the whoop of an owl startled a deer.

A coyote's yelp was heard,
and the muted moos of cows,
Sparks from the fire were rising,
under a canopy of boughs.

The cowpoke snuggled in his sack,
and succumbed to a deep sleep,
Fire's embers were dying,
While he was snoring, he counted sheep.

The next day arrived early
and clear with the rising sun.
He sniffed the cool mountain air
Sweet and crisp - since time had begun.

Colors

I sit by the window, staring out across a moonlit sea,
And I count the lonely hours since you walked out on me.
With crayons, I color my deepest inner feelings for thee:

Red - for the hot love I felt for you,
Yellow represents the golden locks -
That cascaded over eyes so blue.

Green is for walks in many a park,
Holding your hand and swinging our arms -
Is what created that loving spark.

Lavender is colored violet -
The sweet smell you applied every day
An aroma that I can't forget.

We had happy days for a long time,
We would cuddle in each other's arms,
Black is our parting; its cause was mine.

Like many a guy with roving eyes,
I did not appreciate your love,
Green meanies allowed our love's demise.

So here I sit in abject despair,
Looking out our favourite window,
My blue heart wants us to be a pair.

Divine engineering

There are those who believe in divine engineering,
and those who simply do not.
It has been an ongoing argument
between creation and evolution.
Some ask, "How can one reconcile how
an acorn can become a mighty oak tree?"
Over eons, man has created deities
to explain many mysteries.

In ancient Egypt, Rah was the goddess of the sun
that traveled the azure sky,
While in Greek mythology, goddess Selene
drove her moon chariot through heaven.
Zeus, king of the gods, who sat on Mount Olympus,
was in charge of the sky and thunder.
The pagan belief by man in these deities
has served him well over the ages.

Then, along came a new story
about an immaculate conception and birth,
A story that was written almost four hundred years after
the event took place,
Written by men who had been steeped in ancient mysteries,
looking for a new way.
A religion was born to explain why
Rah and Selene no longer ruled the skies.

Falling leaves

Leaves from a red oak tree
Are gently falling to the ground,
Carried on a slight breeze
Their rustling is the only sound.

Soon, the oak will be nude,
And bare branches will rake the sky.
It won't be long after,
That snowflakes will begin to fly.

Bacon and Eggs

Sometimes, we will hit adversity.
So, the next time that you have a bad time,
Think about what people have for breakfast.
Most will have a dish of bacon and eggs,
But what does that have to do with your day?

Stop and think for a moment or two and
Consider the following difference,
Before you cry into a glass of beer,
Or that you consider ending your life,
By taking a long walk off a short pier.

For a hen, laying eggs is a day's work.
Then she cackles and struts when she's laid it,
So that all will know what she's accomplished.
A pig takes a lifetime to make bacon,
Then squeals, which only its killer will hear.

Sometimes, putting things into perspective,
Can help you to get through some rougher times.
Just think what the chicken and pig went through,
The next time that you have bacon and eggs.
So, how do you feel about your day now?

Repairing a Beaver Pond

A large, single aspen tree
had grown tall above the pond,
Bit by bit, a beaver had
gnawed at it until it fell.

The beaver chewed off a branch
with which to repair the dam,
To stanch the spilling water,
before the pond would be drained.

If too much water flowed out,
peril would beset its hut;
Where the beaver's kits were safe.
So, repairs had to be made.

Thrush

What are those sounds that I hear,
Early this sunny morning?
A brief churring trill followed.
By the cawing of a crow.

A wood thrush, flitting thither
Over sun-dappled branches
Gave me a brief serenade,
Watching as I strolled along.

Iridescent drops of dew
Glisten brightly in the sun
On swaying reeds in the breeze
Emitting scents of sweet grass.

The world is magical when
It's in sync with our mother,
But Mother Nature's tears flow,
At what man has done to her.

How much longer will I hear
The raucous crowing of crows,
And the trilling of a thrush,
Or have that smell of sweet grass?

Kitten in Velvet Slippers

Like a kitten wearing velvet slippers,
She unconsciously slipped into his mind.
Since catching a glimpse of her earlier
It was hard to leave old mem'ries behind.

Each was the first love that they ever had,
Smitten, they pledged that they would never part.
Their passionate loving had seemed so true,
He had not expected a fickle heart.

But infatuation can carry risks,
Somewhat like dancing on a razor's edge,
Her infatuation did not last long,
She was not sorry to retrieve her pledge.

A long time has passed since they had parted,
And though they never had any clashes,
He wondered, at this stage, if he could still
Retrieve a love from yesterday's ashes.

Hunting camp

By the light of a bright autumn moon,
Lis'ning to howling wolves in the distance,
Startled by a scurrying raccoon
I am fully aware of my existence.

Treading carefully down the forest path,
My foot slips on an abandoned bottle.
Many expletives leave my lips with wrath,
But soon at camp, I'm safe at our wattle.

We are out in the wild to hunt some moose.
We have limited hunting tags to fill,
Hard to come by; they are too dear to lose.
Love the animal's meat, but not the kill.

Our camp has a tent for four avid guys
Who cleared a forested space of branches;
Building a camp kitchen is one of our highs,
Heaped up, later sticks will become ashes.

Days are still hot until late afternoon,
We shower al fresco under the sun.
The sun is setting and under the moon,
We light a fire to have some drinks and fun.

Tall tales are related around the fire,
Mostly lies, of course, but everyone roars,
Adding more branches, the flames leap higher,
Glasses clink while copious whiskey pours.

Finally, inebriation takes hold.
The fire is doused, and the three head to their bed.
Watching dying embers is our rover,
He falls asleep in his soft chair instead.

We find the rover frozen the next morn,
Where he had been sitting all night long,
In death, just sitting there, he looks forlorn,
The bravest one's system was not so strong.

Bleeding out

I cut myself today
to see if I can still bleed;
My addled brain is fried,
The result of too much weed.

Watching red rivulets,
blood dripping into the sink;
I laugh hysterically as,
Mixed with water, it turns pink.

The wound keeps on gushing.
With no sign of it stopping,
Soon, there's blood on the floor,
Soon, I'll have to start mopping.

Becoming light-headed,
Vision is becoming blurred,
My legs start to buckle,
And my speech is getting slurred.

Darkness is setting in,
I start sliding to the floor,
Memories are fleeing,
Soon, my soul will be no more.

Life

As I get longer in the tooth,
I'm thankful for the time that
has been accorded to my being.
Why do some folks call life a bitch?

Perhaps they don't know how to live
or, perhaps, they actually do,
but are too afraid to admit
wanting to do something new.

Though I believe that it is real,
the bard said, "Life is just a dream."
No, it's not just an illusion,
but quite real in our daily scheme.

And when it comes to wordsmithing,
I'd not want to challenge Shakespeare.
I'd rather make his acquaintance
and quaff with him an icy beer.

As a friend of mine once remarked,
when you wake up and see daylight,
say "good morning" to your lover,
and know that the day will be right.

My view on writing

You asked me to define my writing style,
But I really can't.
I simply scribble what comes into my head,
Essay, story, rant.

Using the English language to its max,
Is a great pleasure,
So many ways one can express oneself,
Something I treasure.

Free verse and open verse are new to me,
What, there's no rhyming?
To me, that is almost anathema,
But I'll keep trying.

The first open verse that I ever wrote
In High School, Grade twelve,
Was called FREEDOM; it's a story that from
Deep in me, I delved.

Then I tried free verse, rhythm being a must,
One winter morning
Overtook my senses; I was awestruck
With little warning.

So I continue to scribble and try
To make jokes gaily,
And about the world to which I awake
Making sense daily.

A Misty Monday Morning

On another misty Monday morning
I was wakened by honking of snow geese
Flying south on their annual migration
An annual event that does not surcease.

The sun was rising in a bright blue sky,
Its gold orb is obscured by the white feathers,
Now and then, some geese would break formation,
Flying high, irrespective of weather.

On the journey south from their Arctic space,
They are burning much of stored fat for fuel,
Hunters consider them delicacies,
Many city folk think hunting is cruel.

But stop and think for a moment or two.
How did our ancestors survive back then?
Mankind has been a hunter-gatherer,
Not just yesterday but since time began.

On Long Beach

Traipsing along the beach,
Breakers rolling onto land,
In the sunlight, I spy
A star amongst the sand.

What was it that glittered so
And has it reflected the sun?
It's just a piece of glass.
Stuck in the sand and shunned.

I bent down and picked it up,
Its surface is made smooth by sand,
And water's tidal action.
- A talisman in my hand.

On your own

Supreme joy and abject sorrow
Are but two sides of the same coin.
These are human emotions, but
Joy is easier to purloin.

In trying to steal your joy, know
That emotion is yours alone.
Folks may be envious of you;
Love your feeling, you're on your own.

But sorrow, on the other hand,
Is something that few want to share,
And though people may try to help,
Sorrow is yours alone to bear.

Banks of the Miramichi River

The freshet has receded.
From the Miramichi stream,
Banks are still somewhat soggy,
As we're searching for our dream.

Light debris litters the ground,
And we're careful where we tread,
So as not to step upon
The emerging Fiddlehead.

This is an annual treat,
Which briefly grows in late spring.
Copious tight curls are plucked –
Their numbers make my heart sing.

Rinsing them in the river's flow,
Then, cooked in boiling water,
They're a tasty delight when
Slathered with melted butter.

Lemon juice, just a few drops
And a pinch of fresh pepper,
Makes a great meal anytime,
Especially for supper.

Rhyme or Reason

With rhyme or reason is what they say.
Or is that without? Don't know to this day.

What is it they mean to articulate?
Can't tell what it means to this very date.

When I think of rhyming, I think of verse.
Reason, on the other hand, is perverse.

Why is it perverse, you might want to ask.
Reason is what takes your mind to a task.

A task that's uncomfortable to face,
But necessary for the human race.

Are we not thought to be superior?
Or are we actually inferior?

Our state of mind is something we must solve,
It's a major aspect as we evolve.

Are we the most intelligent creatures?
Or is there something else with that feature?

There is so much out there for us to learn,
A superior force – we should never spurn.

To explore and learn, as a race, we must,
Ignorance will cause us to bite the dust.

Failure does not need to be a death knell,
As long as we learn from failure – learn well.

But getting back to rhyme or reason,
To me, it depends on what's the season.

The expression, though, is a neologism,
Meaning it's a state of syllogism.

At this point, I think I'll lay down my pen,
To stop my rhyming – again and again.

Parched soil

I glance out my window,
The sky is somewhat overcast,
By nightfall, it will rain
And moisten dry soil at last.

Plants in my garden thirst
For the cool and refreshing rain.
They've been parched for too long,
And for some, it will be in vain.

Summer heat took its toll,
Red tomatoes, still on the vine,
Normally love the sun,
But are showing signs of decline.

But I hope that moisture
Will revive plants in great distress,
And still be able to
Harvest all of them, nevertheless.

Sleeping dogs

Let sleeping dogs lie,
Is often said by those who
Are trying to avoid the truth,
Or open old wounds.

To change history,
Is, however, difficult
Without lying about the truth,
That is etched in time.

Regimes may object,
And so do others who may
Try to obscure what took place,
But scars are still there.

So, when the next time
That you hear the dog comment,
Be very suspicious, and
Check why it's being said.

What is it that is
Tried to be hidden from fact?
Hidden from the light of day,
So we'll never see?

Next time that you're told
To leave sleeping dogs alone,
Throw caution to the wind and
Investigate it.

Time

They say that time is the healer of things,
Including the broken hearted.
But I wonder if time actually brings
Closure from one too soon departed.

Question is: can time heal a mother's heart,
After losing her oldest child
And a family too soon ripped apart,
His smile, though, is already filed.

How does one reconcile a mother's pain?
After she has lost a loved one?
An unanswered question, I ask again,
How does one replace a son?

For a long time, I've questioned why a Lord.
To whom Christians worship and pray,
Does not allow some persons to be scored
Before they are returned to clay.

But daily life goes forward as it must,
Like his Celebration of Life.
In this world, he was not a speck of dust,
But a being with love, ever rife.

Salad time

I drop an uncooked egg,
Into my blender, then
Add anchovies – six strips -
Plus four cloves of garlic.
Then, some Worcestershire,
But just a splash or two,
And some fresh lemon juice –
Two or three tablespoons –
A tablespoon of Dijon,
Lastly, a pinch of sugar,
Before turning it on.

And while it is whizzing,
Drizzle in olive oil.
It becomes thick and smooth.
Pour the mixture over
Freshly torn hearts of Romaine –
Three hearts should be enough –
Five grindings of pepper
Plus a half cup of aged,
Grated Parmesan cheese.
Toss well, and you will have
A mighty Caesar salad.

Snow

Gently and quietly, snow is falling,
Painting the landscape in white
The harbinger of winter's approach
Much to my children's delight.

They scurry to find a hill for sledding
Toboggans are set to slide
Squealing as they all pile on,
All are ready for the ride.

Building snowmen or snow forts is a must,
All part of a winter's bill,
Bundled up in bright togs,
Much protection from its chill.

Bright faces, gleeful laughter seen and heard,
Red noses and colored cheeks,
Tug at parents' heart strings,
Mem'ries savored for weeks.

Summer solstice

By the light of a silver moon,
We are dancing under the stars;
It's an annual midnight event
That we do with friends from afar.

It's usually held in the summer.
Around the time of the solstice,
Some will dance al fresco in the nude,
Bathed in moonlight, hidden by coppice.

There is much warm love and laughter,
It's enjoyed with much libation.
Many young folk come to this to
Quaff libation for the nation!

The Auroras

The Aurora Borealis is dancing
With reckless abandon in our northern sky,
Colours are shimmering green and, blue, and red.
If you listen closely, you'll hear it crackle -
Sounds of static, like when you rub a silk scarf.

Then there is Borealis Australis, which
Shimmers in our southern hemispheric sky
It's our southern celestial spectacle,
With swirls as brilliant as its northern cousin
While sheets of blue and, green, and red do their dance.

Desert Dunes

Golden grains of sand shimmer in the sun,
waves of sand dunes shift daily in the wind,
and sparse vegetation dots the flat landscape.
A goat wanders into view.

I was on my way to visit Baghdad,
then went on to see ancient Babylon;
a short trip into the Iraqi desert.
The trip was not long enough.

The cradle of civilization was
supposed to have been born on this delta
- where the Tigris and the Euphrates meet.
But how do we really know?

Was Eve tempted by a serpent here and,
Did she pick a fruit from the Tree of Life,
took a bite of an apple shared with Adam,
Countless centuries ago?

Meanwhile, the sand dunes continue to shift;
the same as the history of mankind
continues to evolve - ever-changing.
Yet the sand's shimmer remains.

Young love

In the shade of a maple tree
I stole a tender kiss from you.
You were shy, and so was I.
Ruby red lips and eyes so blue –
You had captivated me.

I carved a heart into its bark,
With four initials – yours and mine.
We had pledged our love forever –
Forever until the end of time;
And that we would never part.

On a Persian carpet, we slept;
Woven with a Tree of Life design
on a wine-colored background.
I entered you and heard you whine;
Snuggled tight in my arms, you wept.

But young love, like a blushing rose,
Is a sweet and fragile flower.
It needs nurturing to survive;
Careful attention every hour.
Young love failed; it's now locked in prose.

Snowing

Light snow falling,
Silent,
Cold,
Clean,
And sweet.

Growing Old

How do you grow old, I wonder,
Grow old gracefully without fear?

An old man who ne'er learned to write,
Who worked in the woods all his life,
Cleared the land, sired two daughters,
Was musing in his twilight hours:
"I wonder how many others like me,
Are going to their graves never amounting to much?"

The old man failed to realize that,
Although he had not gone to school,
He had learned to survive life.
And had been a good provider;
Had given much but could not see its worth.
And was now lamenting that his life was a failure.

A Penny For Your Thought

"A penny for your thoughts."
was once said by a scholar.
But at today's prices,
that thought would cost a dollar.

Life

Life is a comedy of events.
We laugh and sing and dance and sleep,
We love and hate and play and work
for things we want and think we need.
Yet, with all our pomp, we fail to understand
that to time, we are like snowflakes in the hand.

My Son

Dad, how high is the sky,
Will it rain tomorrow?
How come people can't fly?

Can I hammer some nails?
And saw some wood, and please,
Build me a boat with sails.

Why must I wash my face?
And comb my hair again?
It's already in place.

How's about some candy?
I'll even eat spinach,
If you have some handy.

Why do I have to go
to bed? I'm not sleepy.
It's still bright out, you know?

Please, dad, can't I stay up?
I want to play fireman.
And drive my fire truck.

My sleeping son, I lay to bed,
I kiss his cheek and pat his head.
I watch him sleep and turn off the light.
"I love you son; sleep well; good night"

On Lake Huron

With vagrant branches
the pine raked the sky;
Its wind-combed needles
lamented a sigh.

Twisted grew its stem,
scoured by wind and rain;
Crooked limbs grated,
rend, as if in pain.

Roots, with rock entwined
held it fast in soil;
Sandy from erosion
through Nature's turmoil.

Wild, the waters raged
on that rugged shore.
Foam-crested waves broke
as to land they bore.

Gnawing at the cords,
(tenacious their grip)
Ne'er to let into
oblivion to slip.

Again and again
tumultuous swirls
Crashed upon scarred rocks,
spray flung far in pearls.

Then, all became calm,
as with morn the sun
Shone, as it had done
since time had begun.

Covid19

A silent killer is stalking the land
It goes from north to south and east to west
It also doesn't care who you are, but
You can spread it through droplets in your breath.

It's a strain of the corona virus,
Recently called Covid 19, for short.
We have no antidote for this thing yet,
Souls will yet die before their final abort.

What was it that set this scourge upon us?
Was it flirting with or flaunting Nature
with arrogance, to cause this pandemic,
Taking it for granted - man's great failure.

There are those who don't believe it exists,
Including the White House's mental midget,
All of the deaths occurring around us,
Thousands daily, and no single digit.

So here we are, cloistered in our abodes,
Self-isolation is what it is named,
To distance ourselves from friends and others
With hope that this scourge will soon be contained.

Flight to Toronto

Flying across the country,
I look out my window at
Ribbons of fields below me,
Ribbons of gold and brown and green.

Really don't know where we're at,
Except we're crossing prairies.
I can't distinguish landmarks,
Our flight is at least five miles high.

We are flying west to east,
Daylight soon gives way to dusk,
The sky turns orange and red,
As we land at our airport.

A long walk to get the bags,
It seems - first on is last off,
So we cool our heels and wait,
While the carousel slides round.

The overall flight was smooth,
The service and food and drinks
Were enjoyable - even great,
Waiting for luggage is not.

Swamp Yodelers

With the sinking of the sun,
Numbers many hundred strong,
From between the bulrushes,
The swamp yodelers sing their song.

Croak, ribbit, and ribbit, croak.
Will they never, ever cease?
I don't really mind their din,
But I'd like to sleep in peace.

Snake River

By the banks of Snake River,
We made camp and pitched a tent.
And under the bright moonlight,
We made love throughout the night.

The sound of rushing water,
Tumbling across rocks and stones,
Was nature's soft music, which
Cleared our minds of anxiety.

Rustling leaves on a soft breeze
Adds to nature' symphony,
As well as a wolf's howling,
In the distance, far away.

Clear water swirls in eddies,
As we go for a cool dip,
To clear our minds and bodies.
While heightening our senses.

It was hard to leave our camp
And it's a relaxing locale.
But as all good things must end
Mem'ries live on in our minds.

Evening shadows

Evening shadows lengthen with the setting of the sun,
As our day draws to a close, and nightfall starts to set in.

It has been a sunny day, bright and with a clear, blue sky;
Temperatures rose so hot that one was seeking some shade.

"Oh, but it's too hot" was heard; a foolish comment because
our summers are all too short, and soon enough, we'll have snow.

Grousing about the weather seems to be a favorite
pastime of everyday folks who are hard to satisfy.

Yes, it is hot, but so what? Slather on lots of sunscreen.
And if it rains, use a poncho to stay dry and comfy.

But back to the setting sun and the lengthening shadows -
Be thankful that you're alive and able to witness those things.

Swallows

Barn swallows are flitting close to the ground,
In an uncorreographic dance
With flying insects on which they feed,
A sign that rainfall is immanent.

The birds' twitter is exuberant,
As they flit and twist and turn down low,
Scooping up a crop full of 'skeeters,
So that they won't sting me anymore.

It's a pleasure to see their blue backs,
And orange-pink bellies as they fly,
Folklore says that hosting swallow nests,
Brings luck and fortune to the abode.

So every Spring, later in May,
We'll welcome a pair of nesting birds,
To set up their nest in our garage,
In our public parking area.

It's interesting to watch them feed
Their young brood, once they have all hatched,
And to watch the parents nurturing
Their brood until it's time for them to fledge.

What will it take

What will it take to get you to love me?
And to make me what you want me to be.

You know, for you, I'd walk on broken glass.
But I sense that to you, that is being crass.

What is it? I wonder, what does it make you feel?
That I am nothing, and my love's not real.

What can I do to melt your cold, cold heart,
Convince you that I want a part of your life.

If I had diamonds and gold to bestow,
Would that make a difference? I don't know.

And if I did have those treasures to give,
Would you be happy or remain as Liv?

Believe me when I say your happiness.
It is paramount to me, not meaningless.

So I'll wait a bit longer for a sign.
Just let me know if you will be mine.

Haikus

The lie

"Oh, good Lord," she cried.
"Don't worry. I'm safe," he'd lied.
Now I'm with his child.

Another lie

Don't worry, sweetie,
He had said, so we did it.
Now I am pregnant.

Passion

Passion had run wild.
Clothes were ripped off our bodies.
Soon, there'll be a child.

Sexy voice

"Sweetheart", she whispered,
her sexy voice excited,
"I have to go pee".

Cinquains

Freedom

With sweat
And blood, free men
Strive and toil, even lay
Down their lives so that we might have
Freedom.

Sunday Afternoon

Loafing
Or relaxing
It doesn't matter which
As long as you are enjoying
The time.

Bowen Island

Snug Cove
Is where to land
When going to Bowen
An entrancing Isle retreat in
Howe Sound

Poppies

Poppies
Swaying gently
In a summer zephyr
Visited from time to time by
A bee.